Little Bunny KUNG FU

Words and Pictures by Regan Johnson

Little Bunny King Fu

Blooming Tree Press
P.O. Box 140934
Austin, Texas 78714-0934
Copyright © 2005 by Regan Johnson
Cover art, book design and interior illustrations by Regan Johnson
Logo by Tabi Designs
Editor - Madeline Smoot
ISBN: 0-9769417-8-3
www.bloomingtreepress.com

Blooming Tree Press
P.O. Box 140934
Austin, Texas, 78714-0934

Library of Congress Cataloging-in-Publication Data

Johnson, Regan, 1975-
   Little Bunny Kung Fu / written and illustrated by Regan Johnson.
      p. cm.
   Summary: Little Bunny Kung Fu pays no attention to what his
destruction of bamboo means to other creatures, until the Great
Dragon teaches him to behave.
   ISBN 0-9769417-8-3 (hardcover)
   [1. Rabbits--Fiction. 2. Behavior--Fiction. 3. Animals--Fiction.
4.Kung fu--Fiction. 5. Stories in rhyme.]   I. Title.
PZ8.3.J6367Lit 2005
[E]--dc22
                                        2005024005

Printed in the United States of America

For my Mom who gave me my talent,
For my Dad who supported my learning,
For my Brother, my best childhood friend,
And my Husband, the glue that holds me together.
-RMJ

Little Bunny Kung Fu,

Hopping through the forest,

Finding stalks of bamboo,
And chopping them in two.

Then down came Panda

And she said:

"Little Bunny Kung Fu,

I have to eat bamboo."

"If you chop it all down,

Whatever will I do?"

So...

Little Bunny Kung Fu,
Bouncing through the forest,

Finding stalks of bamboo,
And kicking them in two.

Then down came Monkey,

And he said:

"Little Bunny Kung Fu,
I live in the bamboo."

"If you kick it all down,
Whatever will I do?"

So...

Little Bunny Kung Fu,
Skipping through the forest,

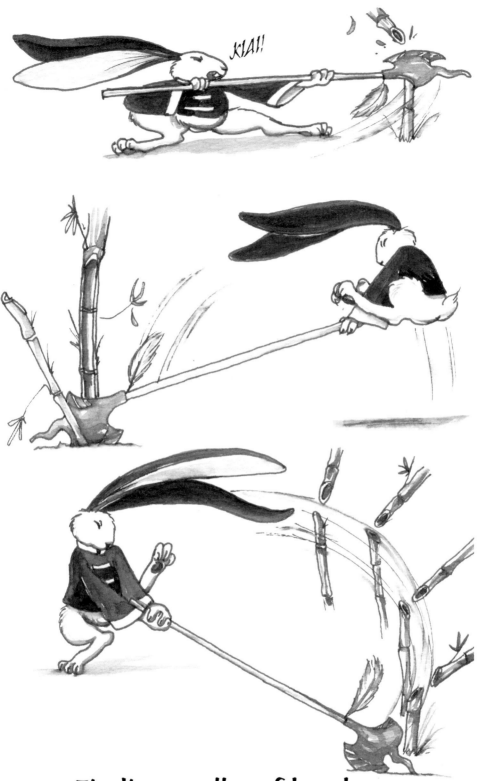

Finding stalks of bamboo,
And slicing them in two.

Then down came Tigress,

And she said:

"Little Bunny Kung Fu,
I hide in the bamboo,"

"If you slice it all down,

Whatever will I do?"

So...

**Little Bunny Kung Fu,
Sneaking through the forest,**

Tossing his throwing stars

At even more bamboo.

Then down came Great Dragon,

And he said:

"Little Bunny Kung Fu,

Why waste all this bamboo?"

"Come with me,

And you'll see..."

"...That others,

need this Tree."

"A Respect should be found,

for Life, which goes around..."

"...And around,"

"...And around."

"Now,"

"Be careful with Kung Fu,
Or wind up Rabbit Stew."

So,

Little Bunny Kung Fu,

Hopping through

the forest,

Found some stalks of bamboo and...

...Remembered what to do.

Whew!